# COMIC RELIEF

Haven't Got a CLUE!

BY **KENNY ABDO**

ILLUSTRATED BY **BOB DOUCET**

magic wagon

# visit us at www.abdopublishing.com

Published by Magic Wagon, a division of the ABDO Group,
PO Box 398166, Minneapolis, Minnesota 55439. Copyright © 2014
by Abdo Consulting Group, Inc. International copyrights reserved in all
countries. All rights reserved. No part of this book may be reproduced
in any form without written permission from the publisher.

Calico Chapter Books™ is a trademark and logo of Magic Wagon.

Printed in the United States of America, North Mankato, Minnesota.
062013
092013

 This book contains at least 10% recycled materials.

Text by Kenny Abdo
Illustrations by Bob Doucet
Edited by Karen Latchana Kenney
Cover and interior design by Colleen Dolphin, Mighty Media, Inc.

Library of Congress Cataloging-in-Publication Data
Abdo, Kenny, 1986-
   Comic relief / Kenny Abdo ; illustrated by Bob Doucet.
      p. cm. – (Haven't got a clue!)
   Summary: Impressed by his first case, Principal Links asks fourth-grade
detective Jon Gummyshoes to find out who is selling fake comic books
to the students, but Jon is not going to like where his investigation leads
him.
   ISBN 978-1-61641-951-6
1.  Comic books, strips, etc.-Juvenile fiction. 2.  Product counterfeiting-
-Juvenile fiction. 3.  Elementary schools–Juvenile fiction. 4.  Friendship-
-Juvenile fiction. [1. Mystery and detective stories. 2. Cartoons and
comics–Fiction. 3. Counterfeits and counterfeiting–Fiction. 4. Elementary
schools–Fiction. 5. Schools–Fiction. 6. Friendship–Fiction.] I. Doucet,
Bob, ill. II. Title.
   PZ7.A1589334Com 2013
   813.6–dc23
                                    2013001066

# Table of Contents

# The Usual Suspects
## THE WHO'S WHO OF THE CASE

JON
GUMMYSHOES

LAWRENCE
"LARRY"
MACGUFFIN

PRINCIPAL
LINKS

**BEAR SAXBY**

**AMBER
HOLIDAY**

**MOUSE**

# Note from the Detective's Files

The name is Gummyshoes—Jon Gummyshoes. I know what you're thinking: funny name, right? Well, that's not what I'm here to talk about. I'm here to tell you the facts. The cold, hard facts about the cases I come across day in and day out at Edwin West Elementary School.

The way I see it, trouble seems to find me around every corner. So I make it my business to clean it up. I don't need this game. It needs me.

The case I'm about to share with you wasn't my first, and it certainly won't be my last. This investigation dealt with comic books, second grade thugs, and an old friend and partner who wasn't as friendly as I thought. So read on to see how comic books and crime can sometimes go together like a scoop of mint chocolate chip ice cream and a crunchy, sweet cone.

# CHAPTER 1
# In the Dark and at the Bottom

"Is this thing on?" I said into the machine. "Okay, hello? Check, one, two. I think the red light means it's on. Okay—my name is Jon Gummyshoes. My mother is Joan Gummyshoes and my dog is Little Ricky. I am talking into a Hammond Pro tape recorder. My best pal, Larry MacGuffin, lent it to me.

"MacGuffin and I solved one of the biggest cases of my career just last week. We foiled a plot involving the school's most popular kid and a video game scam. The popular kid, Donny Holiday, happened to be the twin brother of a dame that I once had feelings for—Amber Holiday. She hasn't talked to me since I put her brother away. I don't blame her for it, really. I have a feeling that's why I'm here.

"I am accustomed to using my notebook. But it is pitch black in here and I couldn't write if my life depended on it. The red light of the recorder is helping me see what's around. So I'll describe the details of the strange case. Hopefully, talking through everything will help me figure out where I am.

"After I was dumped in here, I tore off the bandana that covered my eyes. I looked around slowly with a little help from the recorder's light. I can't see a ceiling, so I'll assume I am at the bottom of a very tall tower. To my left is what appears to be a really thick pole with a guardrail around it that reaches up toward the ceiling.

I can hear loud clanging noises, like metal falling on metal. It's making me uneasy. For some reason, I can't shake the thought of Amber at the moment. I think she might have the answers to where I am and why. I wish I could ask her, but I don't have my cell phone.

"So here I am, Jon Gummyshoes—age ten and at the very bottom—in the dark and at the bottom. Sounds like how my cases usually go. Only this time I can't really see the way out. Which is important for all detectives to know. You have to always be able to see the way out. Anyways, I will start from the beginning."

## CHAPTER 2
# Like a Game of Ping-Pong

The week had started off well enough. I woke up on Monday to the sound of birds chirping, not rain falling or thunder clapping. I dressed in whatever clothes I could find that were clean and found a grand breakfast waiting for me at the table. My copy of the latest *Max Hamilton: Daring Detective* comic book was sitting there just waiting to be read. I took my time, alternating between cereal bites and page turns as the story had me on my toes at every twist.

The author really knew how to lay out a mystery in those comics. And Max Hamilton—well that guy was just aces. He has taught me a lot about being a good detective.

I put my dirty dishes in the sink and grabbed my backpack and the comic. I rubbed Little Ricky behind his ear before leaving the house and locking up. The sun was shining. It was perfect for a walk, sure, but I felt like taking it easy. So I walked toward the bus stop down the block.

The big, yellow sled pulled up to my stop and the doors opened quickly. Peering faces pressed up to every window, staring at me. I straightened my backpack and climbed up the bus stairs. The loud noises and screams all turned to whispers of excitement when the kids saw me. Each one tried to predict which seat I was going to take. I guess I was kind of famous these days. Solving cases can do that to a kid.

I found a seat in the far back of the bus and watched as my neighborhood began to fade away.

I opened up my backpack and pulled out my *Max Hamilton* comic. Then Frankie Flats popped his head up from the seat in front of me. I pretended I didn't notice him. He was just staring at me while I kept my nose pushed into the comic. It was no use.

"Yes, Frankie?" I asked.

He just floated there, still smiling at me.

"Are you reading *Max Hamilton*? Man, that guy sure is great. Is that the new one?" Frankie asked.

"This isn't the newest," I replied. "I'm picking that up when it comes out at the end of the week."

"Where can you find a copy of that? The newest issue sells out the minute it comes out," Frankie said.

I just ignored him. The bus stopped to pick up some kids a few blocks away from school.

"Well, this is my stop," I said, putting the comic back in my bag.

"But school is still half a mile away!" said Frankie.

"Yeah, I know," I said. "I just … I've only paid for half a year's plan on this bus."

"But the bus is free," Frankie said with a puzzled look on his face.

"So long!" I said as I walked off the bus.

It was a glorious day. I shuffled my way to school and focused on the ground as I walked. Ice Man's, the ice cream shop, was coming up. And I knew only trouble would arise if I decided to stop in for a quick cone. There was no point being late to school, either, as I was on better terms with Principal Links.

Then I noticed a familiar face just past Ice Man's. It was Ben Christopher. He represented the fourth grade in the student council. Ben was talking to Jeff Dawkins, the host of the school's daily morning announcements. I could hear Ben talking about breaks on hall pass violations at school.

"Now, you see, Jeff," Ben said, "this is exactly what I'm talking about. How can we possibly have happy students when there are unneeded hours of detention being handed out? Most students are only slightly late to class. Now, I fully support being in class on time—100 percent. Teachers do their jobs, and they do them well. So they have the right to expect the same from students."

That was a Ben classic. He was playing both sides. He tried to please both the students and teachers, like a game of Ping-Pong—back and forth. He's good like that.

"But what if students knew they could walk into class a minute or less late? Imagine the amount of stress that could be avoided. They could just come in, sit down, and learn," Ben added. "You'll see a mountain of creativity and a waterfall of As. It will reflect well on the teachers and help students reach their potential."

Ben straightened up and pointed to Jeff. "That means you." He next pointed to himself. "And me." Then he pointed into the camera and said, "And all of you, my fellow classmates. Do what's

right and vote for me for the student council. I'll get this detention crisis solved."

Ben looked over and saw me chuckling at his speech. He buttoned the top button of his navy blue blazer and addressed Jeff again.

"I believe that will be all for this morning, Jeff," Ben said. "As you know, we have a long campaign ahead of us."

"Thank you so much for your time," Jeff said.

He looked into the camera, "There you have it. Vote for Ben Christopher. Keep the hall monitors' laws off of us and keep pizza on the menu. This is Jeff Dawkins, back to you Edwin West Elementary."

I walked past all of the media and made my way toward Ben.

"Howdy do, Ben?" I asked, giving him a hearty handshake.

"Just fine, Jon. You know how it goes. It's been a really hectic race this term," he said, giving me an even heartier shake. His grip could crack the shell of a turtle.

"Sure, you have to play it just right," I replied, shaking my hand in pain. "So you're focusing on the hall monitors, huh?"

"Well, I'm just trying to relieve the tension that is going on throughout the school," he said. "You know, with your bust in the *Warlock Rule* case and all."

"So I shook up some of those birdcages, huh?" I said with a grin.

"Boy, did you ever. You have the students riled up like they've only eaten sugar for weeks. They are still buzzing from the excitement of the case," Ben said. "It has the teachers feeling flustered. And if they're flustered, then the students suffer with more busywork. You know what I'm saying?"

"Boy, who'd've thought that doing some good for people would only do harm?" I whispered. I rubbed the back of my head in disbelief.

"Don't worry, chum," he said. "You did some good and that's all that matters. I just have to clean it up. That's all."

"All right, Ben. We have to head to the school cafeteria for a brief conference," chimed in Penny Castor from out of nowhere. "Hello, Jon."

"Ms. Castor." I tipped my nonexistent hat.

"Okay, Jon. We'll catch up later. As you can see, I've got to get going," Ben said, as he straightened his clip-on tie.

"Sure, I'll see ya around," I replied and kept walking toward school.

Just a few feet from the school's doors I heard the bell ring. *Rotten raspberries*. I was late again, and I wasn't even trying to be.

## CHAPTER 3

# On the Case

"Gummyshoes, what are you doing in the hall?"
Principal Links harped from his office doorway.

I was busted.

"I'm sorry, Chief," I said. "I was chased by my
neighbor's dog. I had to outrun him and it took
me some time to work my way back to school."

"Can the excuses, Gummyshoes. I want to talk
with you, in my office," he said, pointing to the
door. I sighed and marched through it.

Links closed the door and grabbed a seat

behind his desk. There was a green desk lamp shining. Otherwise, the office was dark.

"All right, Chief," I said. "What can I do for you today?"

"It's *Principal*, Gummyshoes," he said, "and you know it. So cool it with the 'Chief' stuff for a while, huh?"

"Whatever you say, Principal—" I replied.

"All right, Gummyshoes," Links interrupted, "I know you aren't that bad of a kid. You have good intentions, for the most part. You've done a great job solving cases in this school."

He looked at a speck of dust on his desk and eliminated it by putting his thumb on it. He lifted his hand, flicked it off with his index finger, and looked back at me.

"But you can't do whatever you want, you hear?" he added. "You need to be in class on time, just like the rest of the students."

"Sure, Chi ... Principal Links," I said. "Let me say that I never wanted to give that impression."

"It's all right, Gummyshoes," Links said.

"What you did with Donny Holiday and the *Warlock Rule* case—that was pretty impressive. You figured out a true criminal within your ranks. I admire that. But the rest of the students, well, they see you as a new role model. You are their new Donny Holiday."

*Holy banana peels*, I thought. *If I'm the new Donny Holiday, I'm gonna have to change a few things. I'll need new clothes, a comb, and some sport skills ...*

"Gummyshoes ..." Links said.

*... Get new friends, start playing video games, change everything about myself ...*

"GUMMYSHOES!" Links shouted this time.

I was back in the Chief's office.

"Oh, sorry, Chi ... Principal Links," I said. "What were you saying?"

"Well, Donny is being homeschooled now. I'm glad to have someone like you taking over for him," Links said. "You have a good heart. But it would be nice if you took a little more responsibility for your new role."

"What do you mean?" I asked.

"Donny was what we in the faculty call 'popular,'" he said. "He was smart, athletic, and had a great smile. That's why I assume Ben Christopher had him on his campaign team. He was someone to look up to."

"I still don't understand ..." I said.

"Gummyshoes, we need to bring order back to the school. Since Donny's bust, every student has gone wild. Kids are coming in late or not doing homework. A lot more detention hours have been passed out since the whole incident. We can't have that here. We need someone the students can really look up to—a hero. Someone who is willing to take the mop and clean up the mess," Links said.

"You want me to clean up the school floors, Principal Links?" I finally asked after thinking about it for a minute.

Links sat back in his chair and let out a heavy sigh. "No, Gummyshoes. I'm asking you to be the

eyes and ears of this school. The fella you always wanted to be. Find the wrongs wherever they are and make sure they are made right! I'm asking you, Gummyshoes, to be the official detective of Edwin West Elementary," Links said, staring straight into my eyes.

"You bet I will, Chief!" I said, hopping up and putting my hand out for Links to shake.

He just sat there and looked at my hand. "I need you to start now, Gummyshoes," he said after a few seconds.

"No time to waste then," I said, parking myself back down in my seat. I took out my notebook, the one I use for every case, and asked, "What's the case?"

"Well, I've had about a dozen calls from students' parents," Links told me. "They are saying that their kids have bought counterfeit *Max Hamilton* comic books. Have you ever heard of them?"

"Sure, I've flipped through an issue or two," I told Links as I wrote down the details.

"Well, anyways, parents and kids don't know where they're coming from or who's making them. But these kids are getting ripped off. It's making a lot of people angry. You think you can look into this?" Links asked, sitting back in his chair.

I knew exactly who to interrogate, I mean interview. I didn't want to, but I had to. "Yeah, I think I have a place to start."

I got up, got my backpack, and nodded at Principal Links.

"I want to keep this quiet though, Gummyshoes," Links said. "No one needs to know about it. Just figure out who's making the bum comics and we'll figure it out from there. Clear?"

"Crystal. I'll be as quiet as a cube of melting ice," I replied, opening the door.

"Good luck, Gummyshoes. Wherever you have to start," he said from across his desk.

I stepped into the hall and closed the door behind me. I thought: *Stark Park—that will be the first place I check out.*

## CHAPTER 4
# Bear's Boutique

The rest of the school day was a breeze.
MacGuffin and I got first dibs on a lunch table,
which was always a pleasant thing. I saw Amber
Holiday walking through the cafeteria. I wanted
to go talk to her, but I never got the chance.
Before I could move, Frankie Flats cornered
me with a million questions about the fake *Max
Hamilton* comics. But I had no answers for him.

"What was he talking about, Jon?" MacGuffin
asked me as Frankie walked away.

"Nothing, chum. You know good ol' Frankie. He's a couple of forks short of a silverware drawer," I replied without looking up at my partner. I wanted to stay true to my word with the Chief and keep this one quiet. Plus, this was going to be an easy case. No need to drag MacGuffin into it.

After school, I walked over to Stark Park. I weaved in and out of the swings that had kids on them. I saw the shadows of kids climbing above me as I made my way under the monkey bars. I narrowly avoided a gal who slid down the slide too fast and landed right in front of me.

I hung a left and tracked through the empty field. The water tower loomed ahead. I hopped the fence and made my way around the corner of the locked-up skate rental shack—and there he was.

Bear Saxby—he was just as I remembered him. Dirty, stringy blond hair hung out below a wool beret. Bear's face was gently tanned, even in the fall, just from being outside every day. He was always ready to sell. He was always taller than me, way too tall for our grade. But you'd never know it because he was always sitting. He sat at a picnic table. On it were alphabetized and numerically ordered comic books ranging from *Max Hamilton* to anything else that you could imagine.

That's all he did after school every day. He just sat there, selling comics to the kids in town. He was always very thorough in his business, and that is exactly why he was the best at what he did.

In front of the bench was a sign. It read: Gummybear's Comic Boutique. Except the "Gummy" part was crossed out. Next to the text was a smiley face. He always made that smiley face on anything he wrote. He knew I was there without even looking up.

"What can I do for you, Jon?" he asked. He took one comic from a pile and stuck it in another pile.

I noticed a large bag of candy sitting right next to him on the bench. "I never took you for a candy guy, Bear. You were always more of a fruit person from what I remember. Pineapples, I think, and what was it? Leekees?"

"Lychees," he responded without looking up.

"I'm not here to cause trouble, Bear. I'm just here to ask a question," I said. "That's all."

I took out my notebook and jotted down a note. *Candy, what was that about?* We were both silent for a few seconds.

"Oh really, a whole semester goes by without a word and that's all?" he said. He removed another comic and placed it in a plastic bag. "We were supposed to be friends. And friends don't just take off like that."

I stood there in silence. He was going to look at me soon. I knew it. So I waited until he did.

"Not only that," he finally looked up, "but we were partners, too."

"I know, Bear. I shouldn't have come ..." I said.

"We were the best in the game, Jon. No one could beat us when it came to supplying both Edwin West and East with comics," he said. He pulled a roll of clear tape out of his vest pocket. He ripped off a little piece. "What changed?" He placed the tape on the plastic sleeve and sealed the comic inside.

"I just couldn't do it anymore. I don't have the stomach for sales," I said. "I found my detective work more rewarding than the thrill of the sale. I had to do it for myself."

"It's always just about you, Jon. Always," Bear said.

"I wish you could just understand," I told him. We waited out another awkward pause.

He finally folded his hands on a clean pile of comics and looked me in the eyes. "So, why did you really come to talk to me, Jon?"

"I was wondering if I could ask you for a favor," I said.

"Of course," he chuckled and looked back

down at the table. "It isn't enough that my sales went down since you bolted from our business. But now you need something more from me? Classic Gummyshoes."

"Honestly, I wouldn't ask if it weren't extremely important," I said. "I'm not here to beg, Bear. I'm here as an old friend and partner asking for some help. And I know how to make it worth your while," I added, trying to gain his attention.

He stopped with the comics once again and looked back up at me. "And what exactly would be worth my while, Jon?"

I jammed my hands into my pockets and gave it a few seconds. I took a deep breath and then let him have it. "451," I mumbled out of the side of my mouth.

I could see the glimmer in Bear's eyes. "Issue 451? *Max Hamilton* issue 451?"

I looked away. "Yep."

"This must be serious," he said. "You biked

all over the county and paid your entire summer savings for that issue."

"Only 100 copies were made." I looked back toward him. His smile had widened. "With that issue front and center of your collection here, you could easily make back everything you lost when I left. So, what do ya say?"

He was thinking about it. I could see the gears working.

"And what would I have to do?" Bear asked.

"I need some information. Someone is going around creating and selling phony copies of *Max Hamilton*," I spoke seriously. "You must have heard something about them."

"I haven't heard much," Bear replied. He pulled out another strip of tape. "I know the true mark of a knockoff is that the counterfeiter usually signs his or her name on the back of the comic. It's never a real name, of course. But they want to make their mark, like they're proud that they fooled the person. It's some sort of ego thing." He stopped with the tape. "All I know is that my customers leave quite satisfied with their real issues."

I took a step forward, just so I could get a good look at his eyes. Something wasn't adding up. I made a note of it in my notebook.

"Okay, Bear," I replied. I pulled my card out of my pocket and flicked it in the air. I watched it float down onto a comic. "There's my card. Reach out to me if you get any leads on the fake issues."

"I remember where to find you," he said. "I'll get you at Ice Man's if I hear of anything."

I walked toward the table and stretched out my hand. Bear looked at it for a second, broke down, and then shook it. After a few moments, we both let go and I started to walk away. Then I turned around.

"Hey, listen, Bear. I want to apologize about everything," I said. "I hope we can put all of the garbage between us in the past."

He sighed. "Well, you know what they say: 'Life is like a glass of milk.'"

I smiled, "They sure do, chum. They sure do."

## CHAPTER 5
# A Mouse on the Run

I left Stark Park and made my way back toward my house. I was wandering more than anything, because I hadn't gotten the answers from Bear that I thought I would. Something wasn't quite right and I had only a few clues so far.

"Hey, Jon, wanna come over and read the new issue of *Max Hamilton* I just got?" MacGuffin waved to me from down the block.

*How in the French toast did he snag a copy of it and I couldn't get myself a single stinkin' look at one stinkin' page?!* I thought.

"You got a copy?" I asked as I reached for it. MacGuffin pulled it back just out of reach. "Come on, Mac. Let me take a peek, will ya?"

"What? You didn't get a copy yet? What about your guy?" he asked, still keeping the issue out of range.

"He fell through." I took one final lunge. "Come on, let me just see it for a second," I said, finally getting my mitts on the cover and grabbing it from MacGuffin. I took a few steps backward to regain my composure and brush off my jacket after the ruckus. "Geez, it's like pulling teeth with you."

"Just razzin' ya, Gummyshoes," he said. "Why are you so glum, chum?"

"Nothing, just ran into someone I knew a while ago. It kind of threw me off," I said. I cracked open the issue and began scanning. "Say, have you even looked inside of this here comic?" I asked, examining the art.

"No, just bought it hot off the press," he replied. "Neat, huh?"

I opened the book wide and showed it to him, "Yeah it would be, if this comic came off of the real presses."

MacGuffin took a step closer and squinted at the comic book. Then his eyes opened really wide. The cover of the comic was real, that was for sure. The inside was not. It was folded paper from someone's notebook. There were a bunch of stick figures drawn on it in crayon. They were acting out a *Max Hamilton* adventure.

"What the shovel is this?!" MacGuffin screamed, looking from the comic book to me, and then back again. "This isn't a *Max Hamilton* comic! Some kid just drew his own *Max Hamilton* adventure!" MacGuffin looked again. "And not very well, might I add. My kid brother could tell a better story than this. Geez."

I rolled up the issue and looked MacGuffin in the eyes, "Mac, who sold this to you and when?"

"It was only a minute before I saw you. I traded him a bag of super sour gummy snakes and my Hammond Pro tape recorder for it!" He thought for another few seconds. "I think he was a second grader."

I crushed the comic in my fist. "Second graders. Those monkeys would do anything for sugar." I relaxed my fist. "I can't believe I was once one of them. Where did you buy it?"

"Well, he's right down there!" MacGuffin pointed toward a short boy just down the block. He was taking another sap's money and handing him another dummy comic. He looked like all the rest of the second graders—red Kool-Aid ring around his mouth and a bandage on his left knee. I started walking toward the kid, beating the fake comic into my palm.

"Hey, buddy, come here. I wanna have a little chat with ya," I said, approaching him.

He took a good, long look at me holding the fake comic. Then, he bolted faster than a mouse that had snatched cheese off a trap. Boy could this kid sprint. Mac and I started running after him. We were only a block away before I was losing my breath. The second grader ducked into the Grofield Strip Mall. Before I could snag him by the back of his dirty T-shirt, he had disappeared into a maze of kiosks.

*It was going to be impossible to find this kid, especially with all of the families walking around.* I dodged and ducked through bags, running as fast as I could. I scanned the crowd, trying to find my guy.

Without realizing it, I had run onto the route of the toddler train. It wound through the whole mall. I narrowly dodged the train that was carrying a whole bunch of kids. I took a step back and focused on every car. Sure enough, there was my second grader. He was in the second car from the front waving with a red-ringed smile.

I got behind and chased after the train. Without even thinking about it, I jumped into the last car. I stood up and made my way toward the front of the train. I climbed over one car into

another, making sure not to miss a step. I pushed my way through kids, keeping my eye on my guy. He had no idea I was coming. The train made a sharp turn by the food court and I almost fell out. I decided, *it's now or never*. And I leaped into the kid's car before he could utter a word.

"You're coming with me, kid," I said, grabbing him by his stained shirt.

"You don't have anything on me, Gummyshoes. I'm clean!" he squeaked.

When the train pulled into the loading station, I pulled him out of the train. We went outside. It was time for a little talk. I pulled the comic from my back pocket.

"I have witnesses who said you've been slinging these so-called comics to all the kids in this county." I flipped through the pages of the fake comic. "Oh man, this is just awful. Not even close to a true *Max Hamilton*."

"Try and prove I had anything to do with it," the kid said.

"Well, all I can say is a true artist signs his work," I flipped to the last page and showed him his signature. It read "Mouse" in crayon. "Wait, you're kidding me. Your name is Mouse? At any rate, I want to know who you work for."

For the first time ever, I saw a second grader keep his trap shut.

"Okay, fine," I said, my hands doing some searching through my pockets. "You want to be quiet? Fine. Here." I handed him a piece of gum that was in my pocket.

His eyes widened and the gum was out of my hand, out of its wrapper, and in his mouth within one second. He chewed it maybe a dozen times, made a sour face, and then spat the gum into the trash.

"Okay, fine, I'll talk. But first, you have anymore of that gum?" he asked.

I searched my front and back pockets. When my hands were in my pockets, he started to run. He didn't get far, though. His chest met

MacGuffin's forearm, knocking him straight down to the ground. I took my time walking up to Mouse.

"Good catch, Mac. You're a true pal," I high-fived MacGuffin.

"Don't mention it. I just want my tape recorder back for the dummy comic," he said.

We both looked down at Mouse, who was rolling around rubbing his chest.

"All right, Mr. Mouse. I am in a bit of a hurry and would like to finish up our little exchange here." I looked over at MacGuffin and then back down to Mouse. "Tell you what. Give me some answers and I'll keep MacGuffin over here from sitting on your chest for the rest of the day."

"No, okay! I'll talk, I'll talk!" Mouse screamed while trying to bring himself up to his knees. "I work for a person," he said, rubbing his chest.

"Gimme a name," I said.

"There are no names involved," he said. "Someone sends an e-mail to me and a few other second graders when a new comic is coming out. We get one issue of that comic so we can make copies of the cover. Then we make up the rest of the inside."

"You've never seen this person before?" I asked.

"Nope. All I have is the e-mail address," the kid said.

"Tell ya what, Mouse," I said, "give me the e-mail address of this person and I'll give you my entire pack of gum. And I'll forget you ever fooled old Mac over here."

"Hey, what about my tape recorder?" MacGuffin said from behind me.

"What do ya say, Mouse? Can Mac get his tape recorder back?" I asked, holding out the pack of gum. Mouse examined the pack and finally gave up.

"Here," he handed me a piece of paper and the tape recorder while snatching the pack of gum with his other hand. Then he ran off and disappeared around the corner. MacGuffin and I stood there for second and then I examined the piece of paper.

"Say, Mac. Let me borrow your tape recorder for a while, will ya?" I asked.

I read and reread the paper and wrote all the specifics in my notebook. The e-mail address was *holidaycollector@edwinwest.edu.*

"Sure, Jon. What about Mouse's information? Was it worth the chase?" MacGuffin asked.

"It sure was," I said.

## CHAPTER 6
# Over Your Head

The sun was starting to go down by the time MacGuffin and I got back to our neighborhood. We parted ways and agreed to meet up the next morning. As I walked home, I started putting together all of the clues I had.

There was someone out there in charge of making fake issues of the comic. In order to do this, the person had to have copies of the real comic. And with the e-mail address, I had a good idea who that person was.

I knew where I was going. I walked up to the

door and pounded it three times with my fist. Mrs. Holiday answered and the smell of lasagna and garlic bread wafted out. It hit me right in my hunger spot. I was late for my dinner, but there were bigger matters to tend to.

"Evening, Mrs. Holiday," I said. "I was hoping to speak with Donny for a second if that was at all possible."

"I'm sorry, Jon. Donny is grounded from his TV, computer, *Warlock Rule*, his cell phone, and guests for the rest of the semester," she said. "Maybe you can speak with Amber?"

A voice came from the living room. "I'm not home," it said.

If Amber wasn't home, then her Dad could do a really good impression of her.

"It's okay. I guess I should be heading out, anyways," I said. "Good night, Mrs. Holiday."

"Good night, Jon," she answered.

The door closed behind me and I walked back toward the street. Then I had an idea. I pulled

MacGuffin's tape recorder from my pocket and spoke into the tiny microphone: "Donny, this is Jon Gummyshoes. What do you know about the forged *Max Hamilton* comic books? Record your reply and throw this tape recorder out of your window down to me." I clicked it off and walked back to the door and knocked.

"I'm sorry to bother you again, Mrs. Holiday," I said as she opened the door. "The main reason why I came was to give back Donny's tape recorder. I borrowed it last week and I haven't had the chance to return it."

"Sure, Jon. I'll give it to him," she said.

The door closed and I waited outside. About five minutes later, I heard a voice. It was Amber whispering from the living room window.

"What are you doing here, Gummyshoes?" she whispered.

"I'm just here to ask Donny a question," I whispered back. "Anyways, I thought you weren't talking to me."

"I'm not," she said. "The only thing I want to say is to get off my lawn."

"Why are you so sore with me, Amber?" I asked.

"You wanna know why? It's because you put my brother away. Since you busted him for stealing the reward for the school raffle, he has done nothing but sit in his room and talk to himself. It is something about getting even— whatever that means. Either way, he hasn't been the same since."

"You wanted me to take care of it! You told me at Chandler Lake!" My voice stayed in a whisper.

"It wasn't supposed to be like that, Jon. You were supposed to just set him straight. Not make a big deal about it on TV and make him look like a fool in front of the whole school. He went from being the most popular kid to the biggest criminal thanks to you. You didn't have lock him up and throw away the key." She stopped for a second, looking to see if anyone was around.

"With him being home all the time, he's become weird. All he does besides plot some sort of revenge, is read those *Max Hamilton* comics," she whispered.

I stopped her and asked, "So he has some?"

"What? Yeah, he has stacks and stacks of them," she said. "He has so many that he could open a store. Listen, I have to go." And then she closed the window.

Bingo. I had to talk with Donny.

Just then, I felt the tape recorder hit me on the head. I heard the window above me shut. I clicked the recorder on and listened closely. There was nothing but silence for a minute, and then a soft, evil laugh came on. It went on for a few seconds. Then I heard, "You're in way over your head, Gummyshoes."

The tape went dead after that.

# CHAPTER 7
# Mysterious Message

I got home and my dinner had gone mighty cold.
I sat at the kitchen counter, picking the bits
of onion out of the meatloaf Mom had made. I
dropped little pieces of beef on the ground for
Little Ricky to eat.

"How was your day, sweetie?" Mom asked as
she wiped down the counter in front of me.

I picked a few more pieces of onion out of the
meatloaf and looked up. "Mom, what happens
when you have a case that seems to be going
nowhere and people are looking to you for help?"

I asked, lifting my plate up off the counter so she could wipe down the area.

She stopped cleaning and looked at me for a few seconds. "Well, I'd say that it's up to you to decide if you want to solve the case badly enough. If you do, the case will be solved—simple as that."

I chewed on that for a second, the idea, not the meatloaf. If Links wanted answers, I would give them to him. If someone had ripped off kids, then I would make sure they received justice. There was no question about that.

I went upstairs and pulled out my notebook and the piece of paper with the e-mail address on it. I studied my notes and the information Mouse gave me. The e-mail address appeared to lead to Donny. He had a stack of *Max Hamilton* comics, too. I found it hard to believe that Donny was behind this scam. It didn't make sense. But every time I looked at the evidence, it pointed right to him. It just seemed too easy.

The only thing I could do was get the e-mail address owner to meet me somehow. And I couldn't let him know it was me that he was meeting. So I got on my laptop and logged into MacGuffin's school e-mail account. I didn't want my true identity known.

Mac had given me his password once when I couldn't get into my own e-mail account. I knew he wouldn't mind if I used it now. I plugged in the e-mail address Mouse had given me and began typing.

To: holidaycollector@edwinwest.edu
From: MacMuffin10@edwinwest.edu
Subject: Max Hamilton

I need a few issues of the comic that comes out tomorrow. Is that doable?

I waited no longer than a minute before I got a reply:

To: MacMuffin10@edwinwest.edu
From: holidaycollector@edwinwest.edu
Subject: RE: Max Hamilton

> Meet me at Stark Park tomorrow at 8:00 a.m.
> sharp. Go to the edge of the trail by the
> lake. No backup. Will have comics there. ;)

It was weird that whoever it was used a winky emoticon. It kind of took the seriousness out of the business. So I replied:

> To: holidaycollector@edwinwest.edu
> From: MacMuffin10@edwinwest.edu
> Subject: RE:RE: Max Hamilton
>
> Who is this?

One minute passed:

> To: MacMuffin10@edwinwest.edu
> From: holidaycollector@edwinwest.edu
> Subject: RE:RE:RE: Max Hamilton
>
> No names.

I left it at that, knowing that tomorrow I would get some answers. Little Ricky was sleeping on my bed. I shut off my computer, got under the

covers, and was asleep before I knew it. I had a feeling that tomorrow would be a very long day.

## CHAPTER 8

# Waiting in Darkness

The next morning I put on my hooded sweatshirt and put the tape recorder in my pocket. I quickly ate breakfast and rushed out the door without even saying good-bye to my mom. She would not be happy about that. It was time to put an end to this case, so I ran as fast as I could to Stark Park.

The park was pretty empty when I got there. The only person I saw was Mouse. He was leaning against a pole. He pulled out my pack of gum and unwrapped a stick.

"Seems like I can't shake you, huh, Mouse?" I said with a smirk.

He responded by throwing a bandana at me.

"What's this?" I asked.

"The guy said for you to put it over your eyes and follow me. He said he can't take any chances with you knowing where the supply is," he squeaked. "It's this way," he pointed at himself, "or no way." He finished by karate chopping the air.

I looked at the bandana and then at Mouse. This didn't seem like such a good idea, but I didn't think there was any other choice. I clicked on the tape recorder in my pocket without Mouse seeing, just in case. Then I put the bandana on and felt Mouse's little, grimy hand grab my arm and lead me away.

I couldn't see anything in front of me, but I could see a little bit from the bottom edge of the bandana. I looked at my shoes as I stumbled forward with Mouse. We walked for what seemed like ten minutes before we finally stopped.

"MacMuffin is it?" I heard a familiar voice say in front of me.

"Yeah, I'm the one who asked for the comics," I answered.

I heard a slight chuckle from the mysterious voice. "Well, it's nice to be doing business with you, Mr. Gummyshoes."

"So, you know who I am," I said.

"Of course I do. You've made my life miserable ever since I met you," the voice said. "Now you've gotten too close to my plan. I will have to make sure there's no chance you can spoil it."

It was Bear. I knew it. "Bear, before you do anything," I said, "I want you to know that you will not get away with this."

The arm turned me around and took the bandana off of my face. It was indeed Bear, just as I had figured out.

"And how exactly did you know it was me?" Bear asked with an angry smile on his face.

"It was rather simple, really. Simple enough that I could do it with a blindfold on," I replied, smiling back. "Initially you were my first suspect. This whole situation stinks of you.

"I went to your boutique yesterday to see if I was crazy for thinking it. Sure enough, I caught a few clues—the bag of candy for one. I know you, Bear. Your parents are dentists, for crying out loud. You wouldn't touch sugar if you were paid to. But you have to pay your delivery boys somehow.

"You threw me for a loop though. First, you had Mouse give me the e-mail address with Donny Holiday's name in it. Then, you supplied Donny with all those *Max Hamilton* comics. You really had me thinking it was him for a second."

I put a piece of gum into my mouth and chomped on it for a few seconds. "But it was the e-mails that brought me right back to you. Signing off with a smiley face. You can never sign off without that smiley face." I took the gum out and threw it in the trash right next to me.

Bear looked at the ground, chuckled, and then looked back up at me. "You know, I thought it

was risky letting you hang around as long as you have," he said. "You do indeed know me well, Jon. Sure, I set up a counterfeiting scheme. It was the smartest thing I have ever done. With all of the fake comics going out, people are coming to my boutique for the real deal—the good comics."

Bear began pacing. "Today I'm going to out Donny Holiday as the real mastermind behind this plan. Then I'll be free and clear! People will come to me for the newest issues. I'll be a hero for finding the true criminal."

Bear took a step closer to me. "You're wrong, Jon," he said. "I will get away with this. You have no proof of any of this. All you have is an e-mail address I hacked to lead to Donny. And all of my delivery boys will say it was him who was giving out the orders. But you will have to be taken care of so nothing can go wrong when the new issue comes out. I will finally make all of the money back that you made me lose. I won't need your crummy copy of issue 451. I can buy a mint condition copy of my own."

Bear grabbed me by the arm and put the bandana back over my eyes. I struggled and tried to escape, but it was no use. We walked for several minutes. Then I heard a big metal door open and was pushed forward. I fell to the ground and heard the door crash shut. Then I waited in the silent darkness.

## CHAPTER 9
# Flood of Sunshine

"Well, that is the entire story. I have concluded that Bear locked me in the water tower in Stark Park. He doesn't want anything to spoil his sales of the new *Max Hamilton*. I guess I'm going to have to rescue myself yet again."

I turned off MacGuffin's tape recorder and put it in my back pocket. As I sat there thinking about my escape, a small sliver of sunlight crossed my face. I looked up to see that it was coming from the top of the water tower. The sun must have been right over the tower. At least I could see a little in the darkness.

*Maybe it would be enough to help me get out of here*, I thought. I tried the door I was pushed through, but it was locked tight. Then I looked around and finally found a rickety ladder. I started to climb, one step after another. Slowly I inched my way toward the source of that sliver of light. There was a latch at the top.

I pushed as hard as I could, but I could only get it to open a small crack. From the crack, I could see someone walking below. And boy, was I happy to see who it was.

"MacGuffin! MacGuffin! Up here!" I screamed at the top of my lungs.

He looked around until he saw me. "Jon? What are you doing up there?! Why are you in the water tower? Everyone was worried sick about you when you didn't show up for school!"

"I'll tell you everything! Just open the door and let me out!" I screamed.

I climbed to the bottom of the ladder and heard MacGuffin turn the latch on the door. It swung open and flooded the tower with sunlight. I cupped my right hand over my eyes to shield them from the blinding sun.

"What are you doing up here near the tower?" I asked MacGuffin.

"I was walking to some comic stand in Stark Park. I want to get a real copy of the new *Max Hamilton*," MacGuffin answered. "You haven't answered my question though, Jon. What were you doing in the tower?"

I went over to the area Bear had his comic stand the day before. I saw a line a mile long at Bear's Boutique.

"I was solving a case," I replied as I walked toward the crowd.

I stomped past a line of eager kids. They were waiting for their copy of the real *Max Hamilton*. I got up to the picnic table to see Bear speaking with Principal Links. The look on Bear's face was priceless.

"Jon, I had a call from Bear. He said he had proof Donny Holiday is the one putting out the phony *Max Hamilton* comics," Links said. He crossed his arms and glared at me. "He gave me e-mails from the culprit issuing orders to second graders to deliver the fake comics. We linked the address to Donny."

"I'd think twice before you listened to anything Bear says, Chief," I told him. "There's a lot more to the case than what Bear here is feeding you. He hacked the address and sent himself that e-mail requesting the copies of the issue. He also used it to contact the second graders."

I saw a panicked look grow on Bear's face. "Principal Links, don't listen to Jon. He has been here twice accusing me of this terrible crime. But he has no evidence. He can't prove anything," Bear said.

Links looked over at me. "Jon, what do you know that I don't?"

I smiled, looked at Bear and then at Links.

"Chief, I promised you answers," I said. "I dove deep into a case that I thought would be easy. But it was more complicated than I thought." I took the recorder out of my back pocket, rewound it for a few seconds, and then tossed it to Links. "But maybe this can help you."

Links looked at the tape recorder, found the play button, and pushed it. Bear's voice came out of it, "Sure, I set up a counterfeiting scheme. It was the smartest thing I have ever done. With all of the fake comics going out, people are coming to my boutique for the real deal—the good comics.

"Today I'm going to out Donny Holiday as the real mastermind behind this plan. Then I'll be free and clear!"

Links listened to every word of Bear's that I had captured on tape. He clicked the recorder off and looked at Bear. "Well, Mr. Saxby. It looks like we're going to be having a long talk." He then looked at the line waiting for their comics. "Sorry, folks, you're going to have to find your

*Max Hamilton* comics elsewhere. These copies are being taken away as evidence."

The whole line didn't make it a secret that they were upset. Bear was then led away from his picnic table by Links.

## CHAPTER 10
# A New Chapter

Mac and I made our way to school. After Links
was done talking with Bear, he asked me to meet
briefly in his office. I wasn't sure how I felt about
this whole case. It got a little too dirty for me. I
sat down across from Links, just itching to go
home, give my mom a big hug, and take a shower.

"I don't know, Chief. This one was different,"
I said to Links in his office. "Putting away a
criminal is one thing. But putting away an old
friend really makes you think."

"What do you mean, Jon?" Links asked from across his desk.

I leaned back in my chair and thought for a second. "It's just that detective work is rewarding, but it hurts too many people in the process. You never know who's going to get mixed up in it."

"So what do you want to do?" Links asked.

"I don't know," I said, "Something that focuses on helping people. Maybe I'll take some shifts on crosswalk patrol. Or maybe I'll get into some bodyguard work. I need to stretch my wings and work on cases outside of Edwin West. Maybe I'll check out Edwin East. I know the rest of the school is not too happy that I've kept the newest issue of *Max Hamilton* from getting into their mitts. That will sure make things complicated."

"Either way, Gummyshoes," Links said, "You've done some good here, and really helped us put a stop to a bad crime. So we could use your assistance whenever you are willing and able."

I stood up and gave him a nod. "I'll see ya around, Chief."

"You'll see me tomorrow here at school, Gummyshoes," Links said.

I closed the door behind me and thought, *maybe*. Then MacGuffin greeted me.

"Listen, Mac. I know you're my partner. And it's crummy that I kept this case in the shadows from you. I was just following orders from Principal Links to keep it quiet. Plus, it's easier to get dirty when you're not dragging other people into the mud," I told him.

"I understand, Jon," MacGuffin said. "I appreciate that. Just try to keep me in the loop more in the future. Maybe I could have helped make things easier."

He put his hand out for a high five. What a guy! I put out my five fingers and we slapped them together. "Thanks, chum," I said.

"So what now?" he asked as we walked toward the school's exit.

"Well, I think I'll be grounded for a while for missing school and not saying good-bye to my mom this morning. But this chapter of our detective work is just ending," I said. "So I guess we'll be starting a new one."

X Principal Links: fake comic books around the school

X Bear Saxby: acting strangely, candy, what was that about??

X Mouse: gets the comic from a mysterious supplier

X E-mail address: holidaycollector@edwinwest.edu

X Donny Holiday: "You're in way over your head, Gummyshoes."

Water Tower

STARK

STARK PARK

Meet here at 8:00 a.m.

X